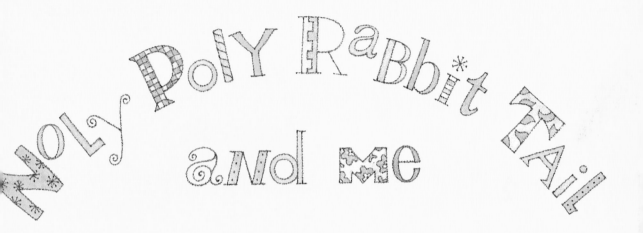

Noly Poly Rabbit Tail and Me

Maggie Smith

Lothrop, Lee & Shepard Books   New York

First Edition 1 2 3 4 5 6 7 8 9 10

Library of Congress Cataloging in Publication Data
Smith, Maggie, Noly Poly Rabbit Tail and me / by Maggie Smith.
p.   cm. Summary: Noly is the best doll anyone could have because she under-
stands about bee stings, brussels sprouts, and scary things. ISBN 0-688-09570-4. —
ISBN 0-688-09571-2 (lib. bdg.) [1. Dolls—Fiction.] I. Title. PZ7.S65474No
1990 [E]—dc20
89-14508 CIP AC

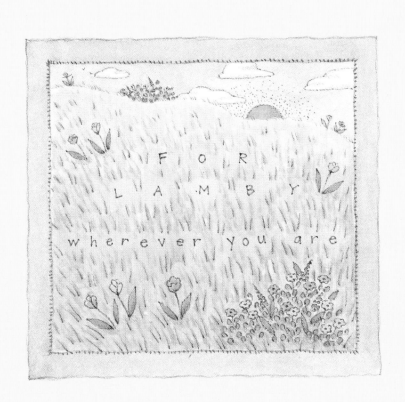

FOR
LAMBY
wherever you are

This is a story about my doll, Noly.

For a very long time,
Noly was my very best friend.

Actually, she was a rabbit.

Her real name was Noly Poly Rabbit Tail.
My favorite uncle, Harold, gave her to me.

For a very long time,
Noly was there
almost all of the time.

Once I patted a bumblebee.
It looked so soft and fuzzy.
When it stung me I squeezed Noly really hard
and she didn't even make a peep.

At nursery school
Noly guarded my cubbyhole,
and at nap time
she came out and napped with me.

Whenever I had to walk past
the scary picture of Dad's ancestors,
I looked at Noly's face instead.

Noly was there at my birthday parties,

and Noly was there
when I had the chicken pox.

When my parents went to Portugal
and left my little brother Jasper and me
with Mean Mrs. Dean,
Noly let me hide my brussels sprouts
under her skirt.

When they came home
and gave me a little Portuguese doll,
I told Noly not to worry
because I could never love another doll
as much as I loved her.

Most of the time we just played.

The first time Dad let me get the mail
all by myself,
Noly came with me.

When Mom told me our friend Arthur
was sick with a big scary illness,
Noly let me cry on her dress.

Noly was always there.

But once Noly wasn't there
for five whole days.

I left her at Grandma's by mistake
because we had to hurry for the train
and I thought she was in my llama bag.

But she wasn't.

Dad said Grandma would mail her to me,
but all I knew was that
Noly wasn't there.

She wasn't there on the train
to look out the window
or to read books.

And that night she wasn't there
to fall asleep with.
I didn't know how to fall asleep
without Noly.

I tried another doll,
but it wasn't the same.
I wanted the way Noly smelled
and the way Noly felt.

I wanted the way she looked at me
with her shiny eyes
that were happy and sad
at the same time.

I wanted Noly.

In the daytime I felt funny,
as if I'd forgotten to put on my shoes
or to wear an undershirt.
But it was Noly I was missing.

She wasn't there
when I came home from school,

and she wasn't there
at the supper table.

I wanted her to come home.

Finally, after five long days,
The mailman brought me a package.

I took Noly out and gave her a giant hug.
I squeezed her softness and smelled her smell.
I looked into her shiny black eyes,
and I told her I would never leave her again.

And from that day on,
Noly was always there.

E
S

Smith, Maggie.

Noly Poly Rabbit
Tail and me.